RAGGEDY ANN'S
LUCKY
PENNIES.
BY
JOHNNY GRUELLE.

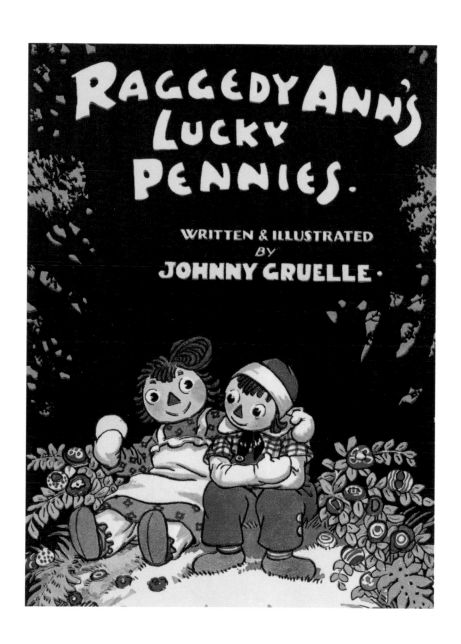

RAGGEDY ANN'S LUCKY PENNIES.

WRITTEN & ILLUSTRATED
BY
JOHNNY GRUELLE.

SIMON & SCHUSTER BOOKS FOR YOUNG READERS

New York   London   Toronto   Sydney   Singapore

Publisher's Note:

Simon & Schuster Books for Young Readers is proud to be reissuing this American classic in the format in which it was originally published. The color illustrations have been reproduced from those in the early printings, thus restoring the delicacy and detail that were lost as the plates deteriorated over many printings. We have restored the endpapers and the jacket to their original condition and, as in that edition, there is no table of contents. The book is printed on acid-free paper for permanence and signature-sewn in the traditional manner for ease of use.

 SIMON & SCHUSTER BOOKS FOR YOUNG READERS
An imprint of Simon & Schuster Children's Publishing Division
1230 Avenue of the Americas, New York, New York 10020
Copyright 1932 by John B. Gruelle.
Copyright renewed © 1960 by Simon & Schuster, Inc.
First Simon & Schuster Books for Young Readers Edition, 2003
The names and depictions of Raggedy Ann and Raggedy Andy are trademarks of Simon & Schuster.
All rights reserved, including the right of reproduction in whole or in part in any form.
SIMON & SCHUSTER BOOKS FOR YOUNG READERS is a trademark of Simon & Schuster.
The text for this book is set in Caslon Old Face.
Manufactured in China
10 9 8 7 6 5 4 3 2 1
Library of Congress Cataloging-in-Publication Data
Gruelle, Johnny, 1880-1938
Raggedy Ann's lucky pennies / written and illustrated by Johnny Gruelle
p. cm.
Summary: With the help of a Lucky Penny and newly-found friends, Raggedy Ann and Raggedy Andy help restore a lost prince to his kingdom.
ISBN 0-689-85719-5 (alk. paper)
[1. Dolls—Fiction. 2. Magic—Fiction. 3. Adventure and adventurers—Fiction.]
I. Title.
PZ7.G9324 Ral 2003
[Fic]—dc21   2002075947

To
Betty Lou Mac Keever

*With a Raggedy Ann wish that her pathway through the
Deep, Deep Woods of Life may be filled with the Sunshine of
Happiness and bordered with the Flowers of Love and
Friendship, and with Lucky Penny Trees.*

JOHNNY GRUELLE
Sissabagami Lake, Wisconsin
July 1931

JOHNNY GRUELLE.

RAGGEDY ANN'S LUCKY PENNIES

CHAPTER ONE

THE LOST PRINCE

"*T*HE *Lucky Penny*," Raggedy Ann cried. "It's gone."

"Have you lost something?" a soft voice asked, and Raggedy Ann and Raggedy Andy saw a donkey peeping out from the bushes of the deep, deep woods.

"Raggedy Ann had a Lucky Penny wrapped up in her hanky," Raggedy Andy answered. "She has lost it."

"My name is Noodles," the donkey said as he came out on the path. "Perhaps we may find it again."

"Oh, Raggedy Ann!" Raggedy Andy cried, "maybe the Lucky Penny dropped near the chocolate mud puddle when you took out your hanky to wipe my mouth."

"Then let us go there and hunt for it," Noodles the donkey suggested. So he caught hold of the Raggedys' hands and ran with them down the path.

7

When the Raggedys and the donkey came to the chocolate ice cream mud puddle they found a young man sitting there.

The young man's clothing was faded and torn as if he had been wandering through bushes and thickets.

As the Raggedys and the donkey walked up, the young man held his finger against his mouth as if to say, "Shhhh."

So Raggedy Ann and Raggedy Andy and the donkey tiptoed up quietly and sat down beside the young man in the soft grass.

And presently they heard, very low at first, as if far, far away, a lovely sweet melody. Then the music grew louder just as if unseen musicians had walked closer while they played.

When the music ceased, the young man said, "It is the magical singing violins. I hear them wherever I go."

"Do you know, Raggedy Ann, when the singing violins play, the music seems to carry me way off somewhere. I can almost see the place—I can almost remember something, but just as I am about to remember what it is the music stops, and leaves me wondering—"

"Maybe you were a prince once upon a time," Raggedy Andy said.

"Yes," the young man sighed, "I believe you are right, Raggedy Andy. For I can almost remember scenes at the wonderful castle just as if all the court had gathered for some grand party. Or as if the court had assembled for a fine wedding. I can almost see and hear these things when I hear the magical singing violins. Oh, I wish that I could remember!"

"Perhaps you are a *lost* prince," Noodles, the donkey, suggested.

"I believe the donkey is right," Raggedy Ann said. "One thing is certain, you cannot remember, so that shows you have lost your memory. Now, the thing for us to do is to find your memory and then everything will turn out beautifully."

"Do you really think so, Raggedy Ann?" the lost Prince asked.

"Raggedy Ann always thinks of the right things," Raggedy Andy told the Prince. "Now try and remember where you were the last time you were using your memory."

"Ha, ha, ha," the donkey laughed. "If the Prince can remember that, then he will have his memory."

"Yes, that is true," Raggedy Andy agreed. "We must try to think of something else."

"Shall we think of the Lucky Penny which Raggedy Ann lost?" the donkey asked.

Raggedy Ann and Raggedy Andy laughed their soft cottony laughs. "Our memories were trying to get away from us, I guess," Raggedy Ann said.

Raggedy Andy walked over to the other side of the ice cream puddle and picked up the Lucky Penny.

"Here it is, Raggedy Ann," he said. "The penny had snuggled down in the grass and was playing hide and seek, I guess."

The donkey and the Prince asked to see the Lucky Penny, and when Raggedy Ann showed it to them, they saw that the penny was as shiny as gold, and stamped upon it were the words, LUCKY PENNY.

"Raggedy Ann," the Prince wanted to know, "where did you get the Lucky Penny, and what kind of good luck will it bring to you?"

"Raggedy Andy and I started out through the deep, deep woods about an hour ago. And we walked down the path until we came to a little tree with queer leaves. And hidden amongst the leaves Raggedy Andy found this Lucky Penny. Raggedy Andy picked the Lucky Penny from the Lucky Penny Tree and gave it to me."

"Perhaps, if we give the magical penny to the Prince, the penny will bring him *good luck*," Raggedy Andy said.

"That is just what we shall do," Raggedy Ann agreed as she handed the Lucky Penny to the Prince. "We have not had the Penny long enough to know how magical it really is, but we hope it will bring you good luck, Prince."

"But, Raggedy Ann and Raggedy Andy," the Prince said, and his voice shook and tears came into his eyes at the Raggedys' kindness, "you must keep the Lucky Penny so that it may bring you happiness."

"No, indeed," Raggedy Ann and Raggedy Andy both cried. "The magical Lucky Penny belongs to you now. *We* have the happiness of wishing that it may bring *you* happiness."

The Prince could not say another word. He put one arm around Raggedy Ann and one arm around Raggedy Andy. And Raggedy Ann and Raggedy Andy put their arms around the Prince, and then the donkey and the Raggedy dolls and the Prince all danced around the ice cream mud puddle because they were so happy.

At last they all sat down again, and Raggedy Andy picked some cones and filled them with ice cream and sprinkled a lot of chocolate "shots" on top of the ice cream.

When they had almost finished eating the fourth ice cream cone, the singing violins began playing, and, just as the music stopped, our friends heard the sound of a horn. The sound came closer and closer, and as our friends sat there a deer came bounding out of the bushes, jumped right over the ice cream mud puddle and disappeared into the deep, deep woods beyond. Soon there came ten large dogs and behind them a group of men upon horses.

Raggedy Ann, as soon as the deer had jumped over the ice cream mud puddle, made a wish that the deer would escape from the hunters. So, when the dogs came to the ice cream mud puddle they could not tell which way the deer had gone. The dogs ran about in circles and barked ever so loud.

When the men came riding up they were very angry.

"What are you doing here beside my ice cream mud puddle?" the large man who galloped up first asked in a loud angry tone.

"This is a magical ice cream mud puddle," Raggedy Andy said. "And we were eating ice cream cones because we thought the ice cream was free."

"Oho! you did, did you? Well let me tell you that I am King Growch the Great, and everything within this deep, deep woods belongs to me. You shall pay for each ice cream cone you have eaten. So hand me five cents for each cone and hurry up."

"All we have is one penny," Raggedy Andy said. He had hardly said it when he knew that he had spoken too soon.

"Hand me the penny, Raggedy Andy," the king cried as he held out his hand.

"But, Mr. King Growch," Raggedy Andy said, "I haven't the penny."

"Where is that penny, Mr. Raggedy Andy?" King Growch howled so loudly it made the donkey's ears ring and he had to put his hands over them to shut out the noise.

"If I give a penny to a friend, and that friend needs the penny more than I do, how can I give it to you? Or tell you where it is? Tell me that, Mr. King Growch."

"Well, I shall make you pay, each one of you," the king cried. "Take these folks to the castle and put them in the prison coop until I decide what I shall do with them," he ordered his hunters.

So the men caught up the four friends and rode away through the woods until they came to a great castle. The roofs of the castle towers were so high they seemed to reach up to the yellow pop corn clouds floating in the blue sky above.

The men put Raggedy Ann, Raggedy Andy, the Prince and Noodles, the donkey, in the prison coop and locked the door.

"And there they shall stay until they pay me for the ice cream cones," the unkind king chuckled. And he and his men went away, leaving our friends sitting upon the cold, hard floor of the prison coop.

CHAPTER TWO

THE PRISON COOP

WHEN King Growch and his men had left Raggedy Ann, Raggedy Andy, the Prince and the donkey sitting in the prison coop, Raggedy Ann said, "Well, here we are. How shall we get out of here?" and she laughed her softest cotton-stuffed chuckle.

"How can you laugh, Raggedy Ann, while we are in this pickle?" Noodles, the donkey, wished to know.

"I was thinking, Raggedy Ann," the Prince laughed, "that you gave me the Lucky Penny to bring me good luck, and we immediately had a lot of hard luck. Isn't that funny?"

When they had stopped laughing, Raggedy Ann asked of the Prince, "Do you know what may happen to all of us to-morrow?"

"Dear me, no," the Prince replied. "Why do you ask, Raggedy Ann?"

"Because," Raggedy Ann replied, "until you are certain

14

just what tomorrow may bring to all of us, you really have no way of telling that we are in hard luck now. For if, in a few moments, the king should send for us and we should find that he had arranged a most wonderful party and dinner, then we would see that what we consider hard luck is really good luck. That is one reason why we should never give up hope, and why we should always feel and know that the sun is shining above the darkest of rain clouds and that with the passing of the rain, we shall see the gleaming of the rainbow."

And as Raggedy Ann stopped speaking, the sounds of the music from the singing violins came down the dark hallway.

"Ah," the Prince said, very softly, "Raggedy Ann is right."

The music came nearer and nearer until it seemed to be just outside their prison coop; and with the music came a faint glow.

Just as the music of the singing violins stopped, our friends saw a girl with a candle. She came to the prison coop and looked inside.

"Whom has the wicked King Growch put in the prison coop?" she asked, almost in a whisper.

Raggedy Ann answered the girl, "There are four of us, Raggedy Andy, the lost Prince, Noodles, the donkey, and myself, Raggedy Ann."

"I have brought you something to eat," the girl said as she pushed two little pieces of hard bread between the bars. "It was to have been my dinner," she said, "but I thought you might be hungrier than I."

"Who are you?" Raggedy Ann asked.

16

"My name is Lovey Lou," the girl replied. "I work in the king's kitchen, scrubbing the pots and pans."

"Lovey Lou," Raggedy Ann said, "we love you and thank you for the food you have brought to us. Tell us, please, do you ever get any of the nice food which is cooked in the king's kitchen?"

"Oh, dear, no, Raggedy Ann," Lovey Lou replied with a sigh. "Sometimes I get a tiny crust of hard cake when it has fallen upon the floor of the kitchen. But usually Ponko, the puppydog, gets it before I can reach it."

"Lovey Lou," Raggedy Ann said in her soft kindly cottony voice, "sit down upon the floor outside there."

When Lovey Lou had seated herself upon the stone floor near the bars, Raggedy Ann handed her pocket hanky with the blue border to Lovey Lou. "Spread the hanky out before you, Lovey Lou," Raggedy Ann said.

Then, while Lovey Lou spread out the hanky, Raggedy Ann covered her shoe-button eyes with her cotton-stuffed hands and made a wish.

By the light of Lovey Lou's candle our friends saw that Raggedy Ann's hanky had spread out as large as a table cloth and it was covered with everything nice to eat.

"Oh, Raggedy Ann!" Lovey Lou cried, "it is magic and very wonderful." And, before Lovey Lou would take a bite of anything to eat, she passed goodies through the bars to Raggedy Ann and Raggedy Andy and Noodles, the donkey, and to the Prince.

Then Lovey Lou ate as much as she wished.

When all had eaten their fill, Lovey Lou said, "Raggedy Ann, I heard the help in the kitchen speaking of you. And I wanted to see who you were so that I might help you." She had folded Raggedy Ann's hanky and now passed it through the bars.

"I shall try and find a way for you to escape," Lovey Lou whispered.

Just then steps were heard coming down the far hall, so Lovey Lou blew out the candle and ran up the hall in another direction as fast as she could run.

The singing violins began playing, very, very softly as the tramp, tramp of heavy footsteps came echoing along the hallway.

A great red-faced man stopped in front of the iron bars and cast the glow of his lantern inside. "Where did that music come from?" he asked.

"We do not know," Raggedy Ann answered. "The music is from the singing violins but we do not know where it comes from."

"Hummmm," the large red-faced man cried, "there's something funny about this. I shall report it to the king." And away he tramped.

Presently he returned and with him came four large men. They unlocked the iron door and dragged Raggedy Ann, Raggedy Andy, the Prince and the donkey into a great room where the king sat.

"What is this I hear?" King Growch cried in a loud, ill-mannered voice. "My guard tells me that he heard music coming from the prison coop. I wish to hear it. Hurry on! Begin, before I lose my temper." And he thumped the table with his large fist.

"Please, your highness," the Prince said, "the music of the singing violins comes to me. But I cannot command them to play and have them do it."

"Silence," the king cried. "I knew you would have some sort of silly excuse. I will see whether you will make the music for me."

"Guard," he cried, turning to a red-headed man with a large nose, "bring in the magic stick."

The red-headed man ran out and soon returned with a brown bag. The king untied the string from around the neck of the bag and all could see the top of a polished stick.

Raggedy Andy, when he saw the top of the stick, knew just what was coming, so he stepped in front of the Prince and said, "I shall never ask the singing violins to play for such a mean, wicked person as you! So you may as well put the stick back where you got it."

"*Aha!*" the king screamed as he rubbed his hands, "we shall soon see. Now Raggedy Andy, you must make the singing violins play for me or I shall set the magic stick upon you."

"I am not afraid of your magic stick," Raggedy Andy laughed. "Your nose is long and red and you are stingy and mean, and you should never have been a king."

This made the king so very angry he shook as he yelled to the magic stick, "Magic Stick, hop out of the bag and beat Raggedy Andy." And the magic stick slid up and out of the bag and sailed across the table towards Raggedy Andy. As quick as a flash, Raggedy Andy grabbed a large sword from one of the guards and swung at the stick.

The magic stick dodged to one side and popped Raggedy Andy so hard upon his rag head it turned him in a complete somersault in the air. Of course this did not hurt Raggedy Andy even a teeny-weeny bit for he was made of cloth and stuffed with soft cotton just like Raggedy Ann. But the king did not know this and he yelled in his excitement, "Thump him, Magic Stick, thump him hard."

And all the guards and the men of the court who liked to see fights yelled with the king.

Raggedy Andy scrambled to his feet as the stick came towards him, and this time the stick could not dodge fast enough.

Raggedy Andy's sword whistled against the stick and cut off a large shaving which went curling away in the air.

This must have made the magic stick dizzy, for it wabbled as it recovered from the sword cut. Then it struck Raggedy Andy upon his rag stomach and made the dust fly from his blue pants. But Raggedy Andy never once stopped smiling. He dodged this way and that and struck at the magic stick whenever it came near him.

Finally, when Raggedy Andy struck at the magic stick and missed, the stick flew close to the floor, in between Raggedy Andy's feet and came up in back so suddenly Raggedy Andy did not know where it was. From the back the stick struck Raggedy Andy so hard upon the top of his hat that it smashed him right down to the floor where his shoe-button eyes hit with two clicks.

"Whee!" the king and all his friends howled. "That was fine." But they howled too soon, for the force of the blow carried the magic stick down over Raggedy Andy's head right onto the point of the sword and the magic stick split exactly in two and flew across the room.

The stick was magic no more. It had lost the fight.

When Raggedy Andy had wabbled to his feet and smoothed the wrinkles out of his rag forehead, he looked just as good as new.

"Now then, Mr. Raggedy Andy," the king shouted, "you have spoiled my magic stick, so you will all have to go back to the prison coop and you shall not have a bite of dinner. I was going to give you each a piece of dry bread and a cup of water, but now you shan't have a thing."

Then the mean king told his guards to put Raggedy Andy and his friends in the prison coop and lock them up.

When the guards had thrown our friends back into the prison coop and had gone away, the Prince took Raggedy Andy's rag hand and said, "Thank you, Raggedy Andy, for saving me from the magic stick. I did not know what to do when the mean king ordered me to have the singing violins play."

Raggedy Andy laughed his soft, cottony chuckle. "It was a lot of fun fighting the magic stick. And when it struck me it never hurt me even a teeny-weeny bit. But it would have hurt you, Prince."

"Well, anyway," Noodles, the donkey, said, "the king forgot all about listening to the singing violins. And he thinks he is punishing us by not giving us any dinner. He doesn't know of all the lovely things Raggedy Ann can wish for."

"I guess I shall wish for some cream puffs and doughnuts just to fool old King Growch," Raggedy Ann chuckled. So she made the wish and everyone had three cream puffs and four doughnuts apiece.

When they had finished eating, Raggedy Ann heard a tiny scratching sound at the back of the prison coop. "Listen," she said. "What is that?"

They all walked over to the wall where the sound came from and Raggedy Andy put his head down close to the stones. "It's someone digging back of the stone," he said.

The Prince caught hold of the large stone and found that it moved, so he wiggled it this way and that until he could lift it from the wall. "Why," Noodles, the donkey, cried, "it's Ponko, the puppydog. He has dug a long tunnel. I can see Lovey Lou waiting at the other end."

So the donkey and the Prince and Raggedy Ann and Raggedy Andy crawled through the tunnel and came out near a flight of stone steps. "I saved one of the lollypops you gave me, Raggedy Ann," Lovey Lou said; "and I gave it to Ponko so he would dig the tunnel for me."

"That was nice of you, and nice of Ponko," Raggedy Ann said. "I will give Ponko a reward for helping us."

"Oh, Raggedy Ann," Ponko said, "Lovey Lou gave me a lollypop. That's enough. I was glad to do it for Lovey Lou anyway."

"Just the samey," Raggedy Ann laughed as she patted Ponko's head, "I shall give you something." And Raggedy Ann wished for a great big large fat weenie for Ponko. Ponko was delighted, for you know, puppydogs all like weenies.

"Now that we have escaped from the prison coop, let us hasten to get out of the castle," Raggedy Ann suggested.

It was quite dark at the foot of the stairs, but up at the top Raggedy Ann could see a light shining through a chink under a door.

When she spoke of it Raggedy Andy said, "I will go up and peep about. Then, if it is safe, I will call to you."

"Here, Raggedy Andy," the Prince said; "you must take the Lucky Penny so that you will have good luck." And he put the Lucky Penny into Raggedy Andy's pocket.

"Be very careful, Raggedy Andy," Lovey Lou whispered. "There are always people working in the kitchen and the cook, a great red-headed man, is very mean."

So Raggedy Andy promised to be very quiet as he left his friends and tiptoed up the stone steps. After listening at the door for a moment, Raggedy Andy pushed the door open and peeped out into the kitchen. There sat the large red-headed cook. His back was towards the door and he did not see Raggedy Andy. Of course, Raggedy Andy knew that it would be impossible for Raggedy Ann and the Prince and Lovey Lou and the others to slip by the red-headed cook, for one of them would be sure to make a noise.

So Raggedy Andy thought to himself, "Perhaps I may tiptoe from the kitchen without being discovered. Then I shall wait outside for a chance to help Raggedy Ann and the others escape."

So, very quietly, Raggedy Andy tiptoed over to the porch door of the kitchen and was soon running across the grass towards the woods.

Raggedy Andy jumped behind a fallen tree and as he peeped back over the trunk he saw men come running from the kitchen door and he could hear the red-headed cook yelling in a loud voice, "Find him! He must have run down the road." Then Raggedy Andy saw the king come riding up followed by all his hunting companions.

"What is the trouble?" the king asked the red-headed cook.

"Raggedy Andy has escaped," the cook replied. "I went to the cellar stairs when I heard a noise, and there were all the prisoners out of the coop. And when I called the guard, I found that Raggedy Andy was not with them."

Then the king called to his men to circle about through the woods and search for Raggedy Andy.

Raggedy Andy crawled in under the fallen tree trunk and was surprised to find a small cave there. He crawled upon his hands and knees into the cave and pulled branches across the opening so that no one would be able to see him. Then he sat still in the darkness, listening. He could hear some of the guards running this way and that near the fallen tree, but not one of them discovered the little cave.

After Raggedy Andy had been sitting in the little cave for about ten minutes he felt something beneath him start to wiggle.

"Dear me!" Raggedy Andy thought to himself, "I hope I haven't been sitting all this time on some poor little woodland creature." He stood up and then laughed quietly to himself. "I was sitting upon a flat board," he said. Raggedy Andy picked up the flat board and crawled with it to a spot where the light came into the little cave. Then he was surprised indeed, for he held in his rag hand a large flat wooden sword.

Raggedy Andy sat down with the wooden sword across his knees and thought so hard two of the weakest stitches ripped in the top of his head.

"Now isn't it funny that the wooden sword should have wiggled just as if it were alive?" he said to himself. After he had thought real hard again Raggedy Andy gave another chuckle to himself and said, "Why, now I know. It is a magic sword."

Then Raggedy Andy whispered to the wooden sword and asked, "Are you a magical wooden sword?"

When Raggedy Andy whispered this, the magical wooden sword began moving out of the little cave and, as Raggedy Andy held on to it, he knew the wooden sword meant that it was time to leave.

So Raggedy Andy crawled after the wooden sword out of the little cave. He was glad to find that all the king's guards had gone off into another part of the woods to search for him. Then the wooden sword swung slowly around and got between Raggedy Andy's legs. It rose in the air and went sailing swiftly and silently along through the woods carrying Raggedy Andy upon it, just as if it were a hobby horse made for a doll to ride upon.

The wooden sword carried Raggedy Andy rapidly away from the castle. Raggedy Andy knew that the guards could not have come so far as the sword had taken him, so, when he came to a knight in armor sitting upon a hard stone crying, Raggedy Andy asked the magical wooden sword to stop. "Why are you sitting upon a cold hard stone crying?" Raggedy Andy asked the knight.

"Because King Growch has told me he doesn't want me to work in his castle any more."

"Dear me!" Raggedy Andy laughed. "You should be very glad he doesn't. He is such a mean person I do not see why anyone would care to work for him."

"Really and truly, I did not care to work for him," the knight replied. "But there was a mystery at the castle which I wished to discover. And now, how can I ever discover it if I do not work there? Just tell me that. There is nothing left to do but to go home and tell my wife that I must look for another job."

"If you are going in my direction you may ride behind me upon my magical wooden sword."

"Thank you, Raggedy Andy," the knight replied. "But tell me: how shall I discover the mystery at the castle of King Growch if I ride away from it?"

"Oh, I can't tell you that," Raggedy Andy exclaimed. "But I have a very Lucky Penny. See, here it is." And he held up the Lucky Penny. "And it is certain to bring me good luck so that I may rescue my friends."

"Perhaps if your friends are prisoners in the castle that may be the mystery I wished to discover," the knight declared.

"No, I do not believe so, for you left the service of King Growch before we were captured. What will you do when you return to your wife?" Raggedy Andy asked him.

"I do not know unless I bring my wife back here with me to help me find out what the mystery is. You see," he whispered to Raggedy Andy, "there is a very lovely young lady who has to work in the king's kitchen all the time and I am sure that she is part of the mystery."

"Hmm," Raggedy Andy mused, "the girl you speak of must be Lovey Lou."

"Perhaps if we get upon your magical wooden sword and ride to my house my wife can tell us how to rescue your friends, and in that way we can find out all about the mystery," the knight suggested.

"Then let us get upon the wooden sword and ride to your house," Raggedy Andy said, as he put the Lucky Penny back into his pocket.

"Why, where is your wooden sword, Raggedy Andy?" the knight asked as he looked all about. "Oh, I think I know. You stay here, Raggedy Andy, and I'll be back in a moment." So Raggedy Andy sat upon the stone and waited, and wondered what could have happened to his magical wooden sword.

Raggedy Andy knew that he had leaned the magical sword against the tree so that the wooden sword could rest, and now it had disappeared.

Presently the knight came running back to Raggedy Andy and said, "It was just as I thought, Raggedy Andy. Skimpy came while we were talking and he has taken your magical sword home with him. I came upon him down the path and he had your magical sword."

"Why didn't you take it away from him?" Raggedy Andy asked.

"I was afraid if I did he would box my ears. In fact Skimpy promised to box my ears if I did not run away." The knight sighed. "Oh, Raggedy Andy, I am afraid the Lucky Penny is not lucky after all!"

"Don't you believe it," said Raggedy Andy. "You just show me where Skimpy lives and I shall take the magical wooden sword away from him, for it is mine."

"I wish I were as brave as you, Raggedy Andy," the knight said as he and Raggedy Andy walked through the woods in the direction Skimpy had gone. Finally they came to a large oak tree and they saw Skimpy peeping out of a window high up in the tree.

"There he is," the knight said. "We had better run."

"I say you had better run, for if I come down there I shall box your ears." And Skimpy scuffled his feet as if he were coming down.

The poor frightened knight's teeth chattered and his knees shook so hard it sounded like dishpans rattling together.

"I believe I will run just a little ways," the knight told Raggedy Andy. "Pooh!" Raggedy Andy cried. "Don't you be afraid, Mr. Knight. If he tries to box your ears he will only hurt his hands, for your helmet covers your ears completely."

"Then I'll twitch his nose," the funny little Skimpy promised.

"There! You see?" the knight said. "I don't care to have my nose twitched, so I believe I shall run."

" 'Fraidy calf," the little man laughed.

"I'm not afraid, but I don't care to have you twitch my nose," the knight whined.

"You had better throw my wooden sword out of the window to me," Raggedy Andy told the little man. "If you don't, I shall come inside and get it."

"Ha! Just you come inside and I'll box your ears," the little man cried.

"I haven't any ears," Raggedy Andy replied.

"Then I shall twitch your nose."

"Ha! ha! ha!" Raggedy Andy laughed. "I haven't any nose to twitch. My nose is just painted upon my rag face, so you can't do a single thing to me."

"Anyway, I shan't give you the sword," the little man cried. "And besides, I have locked the door so that you can't get in."

"We had better walk to my home, I guess," the knight said to Raggedy Andy. "Your Lucky Penny isn't a teeny-weeny bit lucky and the wooden sword wasn't any good, anyhow."

"Indeed it was," Raggedy Andy replied. "And I shall get it back again, too."

So Raggedy Andy climbed up the tree and into the window.

The little man, when he saw Raggedy Andy climbing the tree to the window, did not know what to do, for the window was just a hole in the tree and of course

could not be locked. He ran downstairs, grabbed the wooden sword, and came out of his tree home, lickity-split.

Now, when the knight saw Skimpy come running out of the tree, he was frightened, for he thought, "He is coming to box my ears and twitch my nose." So the knight pulled the visor of his helmet down over his eyes and started running. The knight could not see a thing with the visor down, so instead of running away from the little man, the knight ran right smack dab into him and, as the little man fell to the ground, the knight stumbled and fell on top of him.

When Raggedy Andy ran down the stairs, and saw the knight run towards Skimpy, he thought, "After all, the knight is not afraid," for Raggedy Andy did not know the knight was trying to run away. When the knight fell on top of Skimpy he could not get up because his armor was too heavy, so Raggedy Andy ran and pulled him to his feet. Then Raggedy Andy picked up the magical wooden sword.

"Please do not box my ears," the knight howled. But Raggedy Andy raised the knight's visor and laughed.

The knight was certainly surprised to see Raggedy Andy standing there with the wooden sword and the little man sitting upon the ground rubbing his head.

"We had better help the little man into his oak tree house and put a plaster on his head," Raggedy Andy said. So he caught hold of the little man's arms and the knight took the little man's feet and they carried him into the tree house. "We must put some vinegar and brown paper on his head," Raggedy Andy told the knight. "I remember that is what they did to Jack, when Jack and Jill went up the hill to fetch a pail of water and fell down." But when they looked in the little man's cupboard there wasn't any vinegar, nor anything at all to eat.

"Dear me," Raggedy Andy said. "Haven't you anything to eat, Skimpy?"

"No," Skimpy replied. "I haven't had anything to eat for a long, long time." This made Raggedy Andy feel very sorry for Mr. Skimpy and he took the Lucky Penny and tapped upon the cupboard three times, for that is a magical number, and said, "Magical Lucky Penny, please give Mr. Skimpy a whole cupboard full of nice things to eat."

Now Raggedy Andy had not owned the magical Lucky Penny very long and he did not really and truly expect

the Lucky Penny to work such fine magic. But when he looked into the cupboard, Raggedy Andy saw that it was filled with everything you could think of: cream puffs, cookies with candy icing, lady fingers, lollypops, pie and cake, candy, dill pickles and many other lovely things to eat.

"I was just trying to frighten you, Mr. Knight," Skimpy laughed. "I know it would hurt to box your ears or twitch your nose and I really did not intend doing either."

So Raggedy Andy and the knight sat down with Skimpy and had a nice dinner, for after the excitement of the adventure they were all very hungry. When they had all eaten as much as they wished, Raggedy Andy asked the Lucky Penny to fill the cupboard again, and then he and the knight shook hands with Mr. Skimpy and told him good-bye.

"Hmm," Mr. Skimpy mused when he was told where his friends were going, "you must be careful. On your way to the knight's house you will have to pass right by the home of Wanda-the-witch and beyond that you will come to the giant's cave."

"Dear me," the knight said. "Perhaps after all we had better turn back and not go home to get my wife."

"What?" Raggedy Andy asked in astonishment. "And leave Raggedy Ann and our other friends shut up in prison? I should say not. We must get your wife and see if she can help us."

Once more they shook hands with Skimpy and getting upon the magical sword, they were soon sailing away through the woods towards the knight's home.

CHAPTER THREE
THE WICKEDY WITCH

*B*ACK in the castle where Raggedy Andy had left them, Raggedy Ann, Lovey Lou, the Prince, Noodles, the donkey, and little Ponko, the puppydog, were waiting at the foot of the dark stairway.

Raggedy Andy had scarcely reached the grass at the side of the kitchen porch when the large, fat, red-headed cook turned around in his chair and looked at the door to the basement.

Surely Raggedy Ann and her friends had not made a sound, yet the fat cook knew something was wrong. He tiptoed to the door and listened for a moment, then he suddenly flung the door open and looked down.

When he did, he let out a loud cry:

"The prisoners are escaping! The prisoners are escaping!"

Guards and servants came running from all over the castle to see what the noise was about. Then when the guards found out that Raggedy Andy was missing, they ran outside. Raggedy Andy had heard them tell the king all the story. But Raggedy Andy did not know how angry the king was because one of the prisoners had escaped. He did not know that the king had had the guards bring all the prisoners to the throne room where he sat at his big table biting his long mustache.

"Now, I am sorry that I did not keep the knight here at the castle," said King Growch. "For if he were here I would have had him cut off your necks."

"Then he would have been a very wicked knight," Raggedy Ann told the king.

This made King Growch very angry and he told the guard to bring Raggedy Ann to him.

"I know what I shall do, Miss Raggedy Ann," the king cried. "I shall send for Winnie-the-witch, and we shall have her advice how to punish you."

Then turning to one of the guards he cried, "Go, bring Winnie-the-witch here. And hurry!"

The guard was gone for five minutes and when he returned he had an ugly little old witch with him.

"Ha-ha!" King Growch laughed. "Winnie-the-witch, tell these people who you are."

The ugly little old witch walked up close to Raggedy Ann and Noodles, the donkey, and the Prince and Lovey Lou, and looked at them as if she was very near-sighted. She doubled up her fist and shook it under Lovey Lou's nose and worked her fingers as if she intended to scratch the face of the Prince.

Then she walked away, and in a sing-song voice, which was high and screechy, cried:

"I am the wickedy witch,
I am the trickedy witch, *boo!*
My nose is red and long,
My magic fierce and strong, *oooh!*
I am the meanest witch alive,
I love to give the bees the hive.
It gives me joy to know the window pains.
I put the warts on pickles' backs,
I pull the heads from carpet tacks.
I let out all the wind from aeroplanes.
With a knife, I love to cut out small potatoes' eyes;
Pull the tails of pussy willows, just to hear their cries.
I pound the dough so it will make
The doughnuts have the stomach-ache—
For I'm the meanest witch beneath the skies."
Lovey Lou shrank back from the witch and the Prince
put his arm around her.

"Do not be afraid, Lovey Lou," the Prince whispered.

"Ha, ha, ha!" the king chuckled. "That is a fine song,

Winnie, Wickedy Witch. Now I want you to tell me how to punish these people. And if you can think of something real wicked, I will give you five copper pennies, just as soon as I find a little boy or girl who has five pennies."

"Thank you, O King Growch the Great," Winnie-the-witch chuckled. "Why not send them off on a search for something you have always wanted? A golden apple or something like that."

"Pooh," the king said. "Who wants a golden apple? Not me, I am sure."

The ugly little old witch walked up to the king and whispered in his ear.

"That's just the thing, Winnie-the-witch. But are you sure they will not escape if I let them leave the castle?"

"I shall put a very magical charm around them so that they will be sure to return, whether they get the things for you or not."

"Aha, then I shall send them out into the world to hunt for, and bring back to me, the things you have told me about. You tell them what they must bring me, Winnie-the-witch."

Winnie-the-witch chuckled and held up a piece of string. "See this string?" she asked the Prince. "You are to take this string and tie it around a pint of water and bring it back here to the king. But the water must not be in a bucket or anything but the string."

All the friends of the king laughed at this and the king laughed, too. He thumped his fist upon the table and laughed, "They will never be able to do that, for the water would spill right over the string."

Winnie-the-witch chuckled again and held up a piece of thin tissue paper. "See this?" she cried to the donkey. "You are to take this paper and wrap it around fire and bring it back to the king."

"He, he, he," the king cried. "And the paper must not be burned even a teeny-weeny bit. Go on, Winnie-the-witch."

Winnie-the-witch held up a small bottle. "See this bottle?" she cried to Lovey Lou. "You must take this tiny bottle and bring back inside it a giant who is strong enough to throw great stones into the air and uproot large trees."

"Whee," the king cried as he rubbed his hands in glee, "that is a hard one, Winnie-the-witch."

"Now, Noodles, the donkey," Winnie-the-witch chuckled, "you must bring the king a large pie, and whenever the king cuts the pie, the pie will sing."

"That isn't so good," the king said. "Come here, Winnie-the-witch." When the witch walked up close to the king, he gave her a hard thump which sent her falling against Raggedy Ann so hard both the witch and Raggedy Ann tumbled to the floor.

"I wished that it would not hurt you at all, Winnie," Raggedy Ann whispered.

"Now," the king cried, "throw a magic spell around all of them so that they will return within five hours."

"Five hours is hardly time enough," Winnie-the-witch said.

"Silence," the king howled. "Do as I say and get out of here so that I can take my afternoon nap."

And he motioned for the guards to take Raggedy Ann and her friends away.

The guards took them to the castle door and pushed them out.

Raggedy Ann, Lovey Lou, the Prince, Noodles, the donkey, and Ponko, the puppydog, walked down the path until they came to a queer little house made of sticks and stones held together with mud.

"I'll bet that is Winnie-the-witch's house," Noodles, the donkey, said.

"What shall we do?" Lovey Lou asked. "We shall never be able to do the things Winnie ordered us to do."

"Here comes Winnie-the-witch," Raggedy Ann said. Winnie-the-witch came hobbling up as if her back hurt her.

"Isn't he just the meanest old meany you ever saw?" Winnie asked as she tried to rub her back.

And Winnie-the-witch turned around and shook her fist in the direction of the castle.

"Now come inside my little house, for I have a secret to tell you," Winnie said. So our friends, even little Ponko, the puppydog, followed Winnie-the-witch into her tiny little house made of sticks and stones.

There was one room with a fireplace and three chairs and a box fixed as a bed.

Winnie-the-witch went to the box fixed as a bed and pulled off the covers and the mattress. Then she lifted the bottom of the bed as if it were a door into the basement. They saw many steps leading down into the ground. Winnie-the-witch motioned for our friends to step inside. Then she closed the door above her head and followed them.

"Oh! Oh!" Lovey Lou cried when she reached the bottom step. "It's wonderful, Winnie!"

And, indeed, that is what Raggedy Ann and her friends thought, too. For there, beneath the tiny house of sticks and stones was the loveliest place one could wish for. Chairs with soft velvet cushions, deep rugs upon the floor and lovely pictures upon the walls. It was as fine as the inside of any palace. And the Prince with his arm about Lovey Lou cried, "Why, Winnie-the-witch, it's like the inside of a fairy castle."

Winnie-the-witch laughed and rang a little gong at the side of the room and two boys dressed in silks and satins came in and bowed before Winnie-the-witch.

"Take the Prince, and Noodles, the donkey, to their rooms," Winnie said.

The two boys bowed and led the way down a long hall. The Prince and Noodles, the donkey, followed.

Then Winnie-the-witch rang the gong three times and two pretty girls dressed in silks and satins came in and bowed before Winnie.

"Take Lovey Lou and Raggedy Ann to their rooms," Winnie said.

So Raggedy Ann, with her arm about Lovey Lou followed the two pretty girls down the long hall.

Winnie-the-witch looked after them and laughed softly to herself. "Ho, ho, ho," she said. "Won't you all be surprised though? Just wait until I take you back to King Growch and see what happens." Winnie-the-witch had forgotten Ponko, the puppydog. He had gone behind a chair and had heard every word the witch said.

"Dear me," Ponko thought to himself, "I must get to Lovey Lou some way and tell her that the wicked witch intends fooling all of us."

As soon as Winnie-the-witch left the large room, Ponko the puppydog trotted down the hall to warn Raggedy Ann and Lovey Lou.

CHAPTER FOUR

THE OTHER WITCH

EANWHILE Raggedy Andy and the knight were sitting upon Raggedy Andy's magical wooden sword, and sailing along through the deep, deep woods. For Raggedy Andy, it was a very pleasant ride indeed. For the knight, the ride was not so pleasant, for they were coming closer and closer to the house of the witch. And the closer the magic wooden sword brought them, the more the knight's teeth chattered. It sounded to Raggedy Andy like some one drumming upon the piano keys with wooden sticks, *Clickety-click.*

He shook so hard Raggedy Andy had to say, "Now, Mr. Knight, it does no good to be frightened. We must hold on tight and when we come to the witch's house I will ask the sword to travel so fast the witch will be unable to see us."

But when they came to Wanda-the-witch's house, the knight shook so hard he fell from the flying wooden sword with a loud tinny crash and rolled against the witch's gate post which made a large dent in his breastplate. Of course Raggedy Andy could not leave the knight lying there to be captured by the witch, so he stopped the magic sword and went back and lifted the knight to his feet.

"I knew it was an unlucky Lucky Penny," the knight cried. And just at this moment the front door opened and out came the old witch lickity-split.

"Ha-ha! *He-he!*" she chuckled. "You thought you could get by without my knowing it, didn't you?"

"We would have been gone by now if the knight had not been so frightened he fell from the wooden sword." And as the knight continued to shake so hard he could scarcely walk, Raggedy Andy and the witch had to carry him into the house and put him on the couch.

"No, sir, Mr. Raggedy Andy," Wanda-the-witch said. "You would never have gotten by my house without my knowing it. For I have known all along that you would be here. And I know too, that you have a wonderful, magical Lucky Penny."

"Now that you have captured us, what will you do with us?" Raggedy Andy wished to know as he pushed the Lucky Penny farther down in his pocket.

"*He, he, he!*" the witch laughed. "That is a secret, Raggedy Andy. A great surprise for you two. Just you wait, just you wait." And the old witch ran out of the room.

"Dear me," Raggedy Andy exclaimed under his breath, for he did not wish to frighten the knight. "I wonder what sort of trouble we are in for now? I hope she doesn't try to take the Lucky Penny from me."

And the knight thought, "I know what she will do. She will change us into little squealy pigs or monkeys." And because he did not wish to be changed into a squealy pig or a monkey, the knight began howling so loudly he rolled off the couch onto the floor with such a hard bang all the pictures on the walls hopped right off their nails and fell to the floor beside him. While he waited for the knight to quiet down, Raggedy Andy picked up all the pictures and hung them up on their nails.

Wanda-the-witch put her head in through the doorway and said, "Raggedy Andy will you please help me a moment?"

Raggedy Andy went out to the kitchen. And wasn't he surprised to see what the witch had been doing? She had a table on wheels piled high with good things to eat. "Now, if you will push the table into the living room, I'll bring the soda water, and we'll have a fine party."

When the knight saw Raggedy Andy with so many goodies, he got right up from the floor and stopped crying. Then the witch brought in three glasses and a great big pitcher filled with ice cream sodas. The three sat down to enjoy the witch's goodie party. Raggedy Andy got a monkey wrench from the knight's tin pocket and unscrewed the knight's helmet. He knew the knight would enjoy the ice cream sodas much better if he did not have the helmet to bother him.

"Well," the witch chuckled as she passed the knight a large glass of soda, "didn't I tell you that I would surprise you?"

"We did not know what you intended doing with us," Raggedy Andy laughed; "so this is really a very pleasant surprise."

"And I thought you would change us with your magic into squealy pigs or monkeys," the knight told her. "For, you know, some witches are very good and some are very naughty, and we did not know which kind you were."

"Maybe you thought I was like the little girl who had a curl hanging down the middle of her forehead. When she was good, she was very, very good but when she was bad, she was horrid."

"I guess we did think that," Raggedy Andy admitted. "But if you are such a nice witch, why don't you dress prettily?" he asked.

Then the witch got up from the table and threw her hat upon the couch; she took off her long wax nose and threw a wig of long straggly hair beside her hat, and last she took off the long red robe she had worn. Then she ran her fingers through her pretty hair and Raggedy Andy and the knight saw that it shone like gold.

Raggedy Andy and the knight both thought, "She is the loveliest lady we have ever seen." And it was indeed true, Wanda was as lovely as a fairy princess.

Then Wanda laughed a tinkly laugh that sounded like silvery bells far away and again sat down at the table and passed the goodies to Raggedy Andy and the knight.

"Now that we are such good friends," the lovely witch said, "I shall tell you that I could see you in my magic mirror, Raggedy Andy, when you escaped from the prison coop in wicked King Growch's castle. Even in the beginning, I made you and Raggedy Ann find the Lucky Penny, and it was I who placed the magical sword in the little cave to help you on your way. For you and the knight must do certain things before you can rescue your friends and solve the mystery at the castle of King Growch. But, I see you do not know what things you must do, so I will show you."

Then while the three friends ate the goodies, the lovely Wanda told Raggedy Andy of all that had happened after he had escaped from the kitchen of the castle.

"Now," lovely Wanda continued, "we shall look into my magic mirror and you shall see just what Raggedy Ann and Lovey Lou and the Prince and the donkey are doing at the home of Winnie-the-witch."

So Wanda took Raggedy Andy and the knight into another room and the three sat down in front of a large mirror. It was just like watching a talking picture at a theatre.

"Now you will see your friends at the home of the Wickedy Witch," Wanda explained. "So let us be very quiet and watch. We shall see just what happens." Raggedy Andy and the knight watched and were very quiet and this is what they saw.

CHAPTER FIVE

MAGICAL GIFTS FOR KING GROWCH

RAGGEDY ANDY, the Knight and Wanda could see in the magic mirror the two boys leading the Prince and Noodles, the donkey, to their rooms. There were new suits of silks and satins there for both of them.

The Prince and Noodles, the donkey, bathed and dressed in the fine new clothes.

"Now what shall we do?" Noodles, the donkey, asked.

In answer the two boys told our friends to follow and led the way into a large room hung with soft velvety drapery. There, the Prince and Noodles found Lovey Lou and Raggedy Ann waiting. Raggedy Ann had a lovely new dress of satin and Lovey Lou was so beautiful that the Prince went to her and kissed her hand. Around Lovey Lou's neck was a necklace which sparkled with jewels and about her head was a thin band of gold.

"Lovey Lou," the Prince said, "You are as lovely as

a fairy princess. And Raggedy Ann, you are as sweet as a fairy queen."

Just then, Ponko, the puppydog came running in. He was almost out of breath. "We must hurry and leave this place as fast as we can, Lovey Lou," he said. "The witch forgot that I was in the room and I heard her talking to herself. I know she intends fooling all of us. I heard her say, 'Just wait 'til I send you back to King Growch.' Let us hurry. We must escape before it is too late." And Ponko grew so excited he forgot to talk and barked so loud, the donkey had to put his hands over his ears.

"Oh, dear," Lovey Lou cried. "What shall we do, Raggedy Ann?"

Raggedy Ann chuckled a soft cottony chuckle and said, "Let us wait until Winnie-the-witch comes."

"Here she comes now," Ponko cried excitedly. "I shall bite her upon the heel if she tries to fool Lovey Lou."

Our friends could hear footsteps coming down the hall and when the two pretty girls came in and drew some

large curtains aside, Lovey Lou and Raggedy Ann both cried, "Oh!"

The Prince and Noodles, the donkey, cried, "Oh!" and Ponko was so surprised he tumbled over backwards.

For there, in a large dining hall, stood a group of lovely people. One of the prettiest ladies came toward our friends and took Lovey Lou and Raggedy Ann by the hands and said, "I am Winnie-the-witch." Then she kissed Lovey Lou and Raggedy Ann and laughed a happy silvery laugh which sounded nothing like the old laugh of Winnie-the-witch. Then the lovely lady came to the Prince and the donkey and said, "Didn't I promise you a surprise?"

"Now," Winnie-the-witch continued, "You must come in and meet these people." So Lovey Lou and the Prince and Raggedy Ann and Noodles, the donkey, were introduced to all the lovely ladies and gentlemen.

Winnie-the-witch placed Lovey Lou and the Prince and Raggedy Ann and the donkey on either side of her at the long banquet table.

And they all had the loveliest dinner one could wish for: hot weenies, dill pickles, ice cream cones and everything.

Oh, it was lovely! I wish you had been there!

Then when everyone had finished the last dish of ice cream, Winnie-the-witch said, "In one hour, I shall take you back to King Growch, for the five hours will be up. But first let me explain why I am not really and truly a witch as you all thought. Many years ago the wicked creature who is now King Growch was the general of the army of the beautiful castle. Of course there was no need of a real-for-sure army for everyone loved the Prince, even the people of the neighboring kingdoms. The army was used when we had parades and fine balls and lovely social affairs.

"Well, Growch was not satisfied with just being the general. He worked things so that he made the men of the army believe the fibs and stories he told and, one night, he captured the Prince and I think he either has him locked up in one of the prison coops or had him carried away into the forest and lost. Then Growch drove all the nice people away from the castle and made himself king."

"How very selfish and wicked he is," Lovey Lou said.

"Yes, indeed, he is," Winnie-the-witch agreed. "So because I knew some magic tricks, I had this little house of sticks and stones built here and down in the ground beneath it, all the fine things you see here. We have been waiting until everything was just right so that we could get the wicked Growch out of the castle and bring our beloved Prince back. I knew by my magic that we would sometime find out what had happened to our Prince and would know him by a charm which had been given him when he was a baby. But the Prince must have lost the charm shortly after he disappeared, and we could not recognize him unless he had the charm. So, when King Growch sent for me and I saw you all at the castle, I knew right away that Raggedy Ann with her candy heart could help us—so, in order to fool the king, I pretended that I was ready to scratch you. Remember, Raggedy Ann?"

"Yes," Raggedy Ann laughed. "But, Winnie-the-witch, or whoever you are, you did not fool me even a smidjin. For I knew right away you were not a witch. That is why, when the king gave you a thump, I made a wish that it would not hurt you."

"I heard you make the wish, dear old Raggedy Ann," Winnie said. "And, I thank you. Now, ladies and gentlemen of the court, let us stand and make a wish that we will soon have our Prince with us again." So they all stood and the gentlemen drew their swords and shouted, "Down with wicked King Growch!" "Long live the Prince! Long live the Prince!" Then as their voices died down, the singing violins began playing and a light of happiness came into everyone's eyes and Raggedy Ann's shoe-button eyes twinkled with happiness too.

"Now we have work to do," Winnie-the-witch cried. "It is nice to be here with those we love, but we must hurry to the castle for I promised the wicked king that I would bring you back."

"But, Winnie," Lovey Lou cried, "why must we return to the castle and the mean old king? He will throw us in prison again and make me scrub pots and pans for that old red-faced cook who was always so mean to me. Why can't we all stay here and live happily all the time?"

"Lovey Lou," Winnie replied, "one must keep a promise, you know."

"What will the king do when we return without the wonderful though impossible things he ordered us to bring?" Noodles, the donkey, asked.

Winnie pulled on a bell cord at the side of the room and the two pretty girls came in with a box.

Winnie handed the box to the Prince and said, "Now I must put on the ugly old witch disguise again."

"Why not give the Prince and me large swords and let us go to the castle and fight the king's guards?" the donkey asked.

"Brave little donkey," Winnie laughed. "I know you are willing to do that. But, I have all the things the king sent you to find, for I thought it all out before I suggested it to him. I will dress now and meet you at the stairs leading up into my funny little house of sticks and stones."

So, when Winnie returned, disguised as the ugly witch, Raggedy Ann and Lovey Lou and the Prince and the donkey and Ponko, the puppydog, went up the steps and soon came to the castle.

The Prince knocked upon the gate with the handle of his sword. The guard let them in and they were taken to the king.

"Aha!" the king cried when he saw them. "Call every one in here for we are going to have some fun. If they have not brought back all the wonderful things I sent them for, I shall throw them into prison for the rest of their lives. And I shall give the witch the hardest thump she ever got."

"O King Growch the Great," Winnie-the-witch said in a squeaky voice; "you see that good fortune has come to these captives. They not only have brought you the wonderful things, but they have found a place where they could all get beautiful new clothing for nothing."

"I shall have to discover that place," the king cried. "First show me the pint of water carried by the string."

So the Prince put the box upon the floor and opened it. He had no idea what he should find inside, but he caught hold of the end of the string and lifted it and out of the box came a large square piece of ice. The Prince carried it and placed it before the king.

"Pooh," the king said, "there wasn't anything so wonderful in that. Just an old cake of ice. Why didn't I think of that and make you bring something else? Well," he continued peevishly, "go on. Show me the piece of tissue paper filled with fire. But remember, if the paper is scorched even a teeny-weeny bit, into the prison coop you go." The Prince drew the piece of tissue paper from the box and carried it to the king.

"Ha!" the king cried, "I can see the fire shining through the thin paper. You have really brought me fire in the paper and it is not scorched at all. It isn't even warm." And the king unwrapped the tissue paper and out flew four fireflies.

The fireflies flew around the king's face and one crawled across his red nose. This made the king so very angry that he hopped about and called for his guards to bring a fly swatter. But before the guards came back, the fireflies had flown to the ceiling and escaped.

"That was silly to expect real-for-sure fire in a piece of tissue paper. I've a notion to give some one a hard thump because I didn't think of that sooner." And as one of the fat guards was standing close, the king gave him such a hard crack it sent the guard tumbling head over heels.

"Now! have you the giant in the bottle?" the mean king yelled. "And if I find that this is some silly sort of common thing which I should have thought of, I shall give you each a thump besides putting you all in the coop."

"O great King Growch?" Winnie-the-witch said, "the giant is really in the little bottle, but we must not open it within the castle. Remember, this giant can hurl great rocks and throw down the largest of trees. We must go outside."

"I shall not go to that trouble," King Growch cried. "You have fooled me with silly little things which I should have thought of myself. Any silly person could think of those things."

"But you didn't think of them," Raggedy Ann said. "So you must be sillier than everyone else."

"What's that?" King Growch howled. "How dare you call the great King Growch silly? Just for that you shall all go back into the prison coop. Guards, seize them and throw them into the prison coop and put that ugly old witch in with them."

And even though the Prince and the donkey put up a valiant struggle the guards were too many for them and they were dragged and carried down the stone steps and locked in another prison coop.

"Now," the guards laughed, "you shall never escape from this coop."

CHAPTER SIX

ADVENTURES ON SWORDBACK

RAGGEDY ANDY, while he watched the magic mirror, could hardly sit still and he wished to return to the castle right away so that he could rescue his friends. But the lovely witch said to him: "No, Raggedy Andy. You would fail if you returned now. But be of good cheer, for Raggedy Ann, with her Magical Wishing Pebble and her candy heart will see that she and all the others do not miss food. And they have the singing violins to keep them cheery. You and the knight must continue on until you reach the knight's home, for the knight's wife must be at the castle when the mystery is solved."

So the lovely witch gave Raggedy Andy a little basket filled with nice things to eat. And the basket, being a magical basket, whenever it was emptied always filled right up again.

So Raggedy Andy bolted the knight's helmet back upon

his head and after thanking the lovely witch, he and the knight climbed upon the magical sword and sailed away.

After riding a long way upon the magical wooden sword, Raggedy Andy knew they must be getting close to the giant's cave. And as he could feel the knight's legs shaking hard, Raggedy Andy thought he would stop and rest awhile. So he and the knight stopped beneath a tree and Raggedy Andy took the cover from the basket and was just about to give the knight a lovely fat cream puff when a rude voice right in back of them cried:

"Aha! I see you have some goodies in that basket. Give me the basket so that I may eat them all."

"We will give you a lovely cream puff if you wish one," Raggedy Andy said as he turned around and saw a Snarlyboodle standing there.

"I do not want *one*," the Snarlyboodle cried as loudly as he could. "I want the whole basketful."

"But we won't give you the whole basketful," the knight said. "It's a present from the witch and we have to eat as we ride along on Raggedy Andy's magical sword. Besides, Raggedy Andy has a Lucky Penny so you'd better be careful."

"*AHAAAAAA*," the Snarlyboodle cried. "So you have a Lucky Penny and a magical sword too. Then hand them to me with the basket, for I want all of them."

"You are so rude we shall not even give you one cream puff. And I am sure we shall not give you the Lucky Penny nor the magic sword either."

"Then I shall have to take them from you," the Snarlyboodle yelled as he snatched the basket from Raggedy Andy's hands.

Raggedy Andy was so surprised that a perfect stranger should do anything like that, he just stood there staring at the Snarlyboodle! But the knight immediately took the basket away from the Snarlyboodle. Then the Snarlyboodle took the basket away from the knight. And Raggedy Andy took it away from the Snarlyboodle. Then the Snarlyboodle took the basket away from Raggedy Andy again and the knight said, "This will never do, Snarlyboodle. We must fight to see who gets the magic basket."

"I sha'n't fight," the Snarlyboodle cried. "But I will wrestle."

So the knight and the Snarlyboodle wrestled and tussled and tussled and pulled and tussled some more, but neither could wrestle better than the other.

"You and I will have to wrestle," the Snarlyboodle told Raggedy Andy after he had rested awhile.

So Raggedy Andy rolled up his sleeves and wrestled with the Snarlyboodle until finally the Snarlyboodle wrestled so well that he sat on top of Raggedy Andy. "Now hand me the basket of goodies, the Lucky Penny, and the magical wooden sword," the Snarlyboodle said to the knight. "Then I will hop off Raggedy Andy and run home with them."

The knight was just about to obey when Raggedy Andy cried, "Don't do it, Mr. Knight. He hasn't wrestled me enough. Just as soon as I rest awhile I shall wrestle him harder than ever."

So the knight gave Raggedy Andy a lovely cream puff to eat while the Snarlyboodle was sitting on top of him, and because he did not wish to be selfish, the knight gave the Snarlyboodle one, too.

"My! But cream puffs are good," the Snarlyboodle cried as he sat upon Raggedy Andy and ate. "I shall wrestle better than ever after tasting the cream puff because I want the basket more than I did before."

Then when the Snarlyboodle had finished eating his cream puff, instead of getting off Raggedy Andy so that Raggedy Andy could wrestle him, the Snarlyboodle just sat there and would not budge.

"If you do not get off Raggedy Andy, how do you expect him to get up and wrestle?" the knight asked the Snarlyboodle.

Of course the Snarlyboodle could not answer this, because it was too hard to answer. So he had to get off Raggedy Andy to be wrestled.

Raggedy Andy took the Lucky Penny and rubbed it on his arms. Then you should have seen how the Snarlyboodle and Raggedy Andy wrestled; up and down, this way and that, until finally Raggedy Andy wrestled the best. "Now Raggedy Andy wins the sword, the Lucky Penny and the magic basket," the knight said. And of course, the Snarlyboodle had to admit that this was very true.

"We must leave you, Snarlyboodle," the knight said, "for we have a long way to go before we come to my house."

"I wish that I could think of a good way to take the basket, the Lucky Penny and the sword away from you," the Snarlyboodle told them, "for I should love to have the wooden sword to ride upon and the magic basket of goodies to eat when I grew tired of riding upon the sword."

"I am sorry that you cannot think of any way," the knight said, politely. "But you see, they belong to

Raggedy Andy and even I wouldn't try to think of a way to take them from him."

"I tell you what I wish," the Snarlyboodle said. "I wish that Raggedy Andy had three magic baskets, three Lucky Pennies, and three magic swords. Then maybe he would give you one and give me one."

"Indeed I would," Raggedy Andy laughed. "But I only have one, so I cannot give two away. But I will give you all the goodies left in the basket and you can sit here and eat as much as you wish."

"Thank you," the Snarlyboodle said, his eyes shining with happiness. "But I have changed my mind now. I would not care to have all the goodies."

"Oh! that will be all right," Raggedy Andy laughed again. "The magic basket will fill up again."

So the Snarlyboodle said, "Please," and Raggedy Andy piled goodies all about the Snarlyboodle until he had enough to keep him eating for two hours, even if he ate very fast.

Then Raggedy Andy and the knight shook hands with the Snarlyboodle and left him enjoying the goodies.

"I think that was a lot of fun wrestling with the Snarlyboodle," the knight said as he and Raggedy Andy rode away on the wooden sword.

"So did I," Raggedy Andy replied. "But at first I thought surely the Snarlyboodle was going to wrestle the best, but the Lucky Penny helped me win. Anyway, even if the Snarlyboodle was rude when we first met him, I am glad that we treated him with kindness for perhaps now the Snarlyboodle will be much better mannered."

And, although Raggedy Andy did not know it, both

he and the knight were going to be very glad they had been generous with the Snarlyboodle.

After Raggedy Andy and the knight had ridden almost three minutes, the wooden sword came to a stop.

"I feel very shaky," the knight said. "And look, Raggedy Andy. There is a large cave. Oh, deary me! Oh, deary me! I just know it is the giant's cave. Get out the Lucky Penny and ask it what we shall do."

"We shall wait and see," Raggedy Andy said. "Stop shaking. You sound like two dishpans rattling together. The magical wooden sword stopped here, so it must know what it is doing, even if *we* don't."

"O-o-oh! Listen!" the knight cried.

From the large cave came a great deep, deep voice, "*Fee-fi-fo-fum.*"

"It's the giant," Raggedy Andy said.

"I know it," the knight cried. "Oh! why did we come this way? Let us fly."

"*Fee-fi-fo-fummmm,*" the giant howled, much louder this time.

"Do you think he smells us, Raggedy Andy?" the knight asked, his teeth clicking as if he were standing in cold water.

"I do not believe so," Raggedy Andy replied. "I am stuffed with nice clean white cotton and he can't smell me."

"Yes, but maybe he smells the oil I put on the hinges of my armor," the knight said. Just then the giant came out of the cave. He was so large, he used wagon wheels for buttons on his pants.

"I'll hide behind you," the knight whispered to

Raggedy Andy. "If the giant sees me, he may think I am Jack the Giant Killer and become frightened and run back in the cave."

Raggedy Andy had to laugh at this, but he let the knight hide behind him, and pretended there wasn't anyone with him.

"Hmmm!" the giant mused as he put on his spectacles and looked at Raggedy Andy. "I believe you are trying to keep a secret from me Raggedy Andy. What are you hiding behind you?"

"It's only a knight," Raggedy Andy replied.

The giant thought Raggedy Andy meant night and he howled, "You are trying to fool me, that's what. How can there be a night in the day time? Just you tell me that."

And Raggedy Andy laughed so hard he fell down, and then the giant discovered the knight.

"I thought maybe you would think that I was Jack the Giant Killer if you saw me, and you might be frightened," the knight said.

"What makes him rattle that way and click his teeth together, Raggedy Andy?" the giant wished to know.

"Maybe he's getting ready to bite you," Raggedy Andy replied. He did not wish the giant to know how frightened the knight really was.

When the giant heard this, he drew away from the knight and walked all around him. "Bark like a dog," Raggedy Andy whispered to the knight; "then perhaps the giant will run back into his cave and we can escape."

The knight tried to bark like a dog, but he was so frightened he could only squeak a little bit.

"Ha!" the giant said as he sat down and looked at Raggedy Andy and the knight, "who's afraid of him? Just tell me that. Who's afraid? That's what I want to know."

"I don't believe you are a real giant, anyhow," the knight said.

"Ha! Don't you fool yourself," the giant laughed. "I'm the biggest giant around here, I'll tell you that myself. What makes you think I am not a real giant?"

"Because," the knight replied, "whoever heard of a bald-headed giant?"

"Ha!" the giant laughed. "I'm not entirely bald-headed. Beside, haven't giants got a right to be bald-headed just as well as anyone else?"

"Maybe they have," the knight replied. "But, bald-headed giants are not as good as giants with a whole lot of hair. I know that."

The giant picked up a large tree trunk. Then he stood up and put the tree trunk upon his shoulder. "If you think I am not as good as the next giant, just you knock this chip off my shoulder. Knock it off if you dare."

"How can he knock it off your shoulder when he can't reach that high?" Raggedy Andy asked.

So the giant put the tree trunk upon the knight's shoulder, but the knight couldn't hold up the tree trunk; it was too heavy.

"See! He lies down," the giant cried as he danced about. "He's a scaredy calf."

"No, he isn't," Raggedy Andy answered. "You mustn't put such a large chip on his shoulder. He isn't as big as you are."

So the giant put a small chip on the knight's shoulder and then knocked it off.

"You'd better not do that again," the knight said. "First thing you know I'll get mad." But the giant did it again and the knight hit him upon the ankle. Then the giant ran after the knight. And, when the giant grew tired of chasing the knight, the knight chased the giant.

And, while the knight was chasing the giant, the giant fell down, and, before the giant could get up, the knight tied a string around the giant's nose and brought him back to Raggedy Andy. The knight tied the string to a tree and sat down to rest. Before he did this, however, the knight walked up to the giant and pretended that he was turning a key in a lock. *"Tick tock, the door is locked,"* the knight said.

"Hh!" the giant cried, "I don't see any door at all."

"Of course not," Raggedy Andy explained, "because there isn't any door. But when anyone says that, you can't get away because if you did, it wouldn't be fair."

"I want to be fair," the giant replied, "but I do not like this string so tight around my nose."

Raggedy Andy loosened the string around the giant's nose and then they all sat down.

"Do you like children?" Raggedy Andy asked the giant, just to have something to talk about.

"Oh, yes," the giant replied. "I am very fond of children. But I like little girls better than I like little boys."

"Dear me! You should be ashamed to say that," Raggedy Andy told the giant.

"I don't see why," the giant laughed. "Little boys

73

are made of snips and snails and puppydog tails. And little girls are made of sugar and spice and all things nice. That's why I like little girls best."

"And do you eat men, too?" the knight asked as he began to shake again.

"Only gingerbread men," the giant replied. "I am very fond of gingerbread men with raisin eyes."

"I'm glad you are fond only of gingerbread men," the knight decided, "now I can stop shaking."

"Oh, I just happened to think," the giant laughed. "I'll bet a nickel you thought I ate people. Now didn't you?"

"Yes, we did," Raggedy Andy admitted.

"How silly!" the giant said. "Why, giants are kinder than other people, because they have larger hearts. So, whenever you see a giant you may know he is really a nice person. That is why I was playing so hard with the knight. It is because I like everybody." When the knight heard this he untied the string completely from the giant's nose.

"I thought we were fighting all the time," the knight said. "That's why I was frightened."

"There is no reason to be frightened of me," the giant laughed heartily. "And now," he continued, "it is about time for school to let out, so if you will come into my · cave you may see all the children who live with me. You see," the giant explained, "'way off through the woods there is a large castle and there was a great deal of trouble there a few years ago, so I took all the children to live with me."

Raggedy Andy and the knight thought that was a nice

idea. They followed the giant into the cave and watched
the children march down a long stairway from the
schoolroom.

All the children went into the dining room and sat
at a long table.

The giant and the teachers and Raggedy Andy and
the knight sat at the head of the table. Then the giant
said grace and rang a bell which tinkled back in the
kitchen. Soon a strange thing happened. The edge of
the long table began to move just like a moving side-
walk, out into the kitchen and around the table again,
and, as it came back into the dining room each one of the
children had his food brought right to him on the moving
table.

Then you should have heard the clatter of knives and

forks and spoons as the children enjoyed the lovely dinner. They laughed and talked and had as nice a time as if they were all at a fine birthday party. After every one had had three dishes of ice cream, the head teacher rang a bell and all the children romped out of the cave to play, for school was over for the day.

"I think you are a very nice giant," Raggedy Andy said. And indeed this was quite true.

"Some day," the giant told them, "some one will come along who will solve the mystery at the great white castle. Then all the children can return there."

Upon hearing this, the knight told the kindly giant all about Raggedy Andy escaping from the castle of the wicked King Growch and how they were on their way to his house to get his wife.

"When you reach your home and get your wife, I wish you would come back this way," the giant said. "Perhaps I may be able to help you."

"Thank you," Raggedy Andy told the giant.

Just as Raggedy Andy and the knight were shaking hands with the giant, all of the children stopped their play and ran into the cave crying, "Here comes the Boliver! Here comes the Boliver!"

"Excuse me," the giant said hurrying into the cave so fast that he almost pulled the cave in behind him.

The knight would have followed the giant, but his knees shook together so hard he could not move. So he had to stay behind with Raggedy Andy until the Boliver came running up.

"Ha, Raggedy Andy!" the Boliver cried. "Where is the giant?"

"He ran away, Mr. Boliver," Raggedy Andy answered very politely.

"Huh! Don't I know that? Wouldn't he be here if he had not run away?" the Boliver asked as he rolled his googly eyes.

"Then if you knew it, you shouldn't have asked," Raggedy Andy said. "You are all out of breath from running so hard and you should have caught your breath before you wasted it asking silly questions."

What Raggedy Andy said made the Boliver very, very angry; so angry, indeed, that he twisted his tail into a hard knot and couldn't untie it.

"See what you've done, Raggedy Andy?" the Boliver howled. "Now you must untie my tail."

"If you wish me to untie your tail you will have to say 'Please,'" Raggedy Andy answered. "You cannot expect people to do things for you unless you are polite." So, when the Boliver had said "Please," Raggedy Andy untied the hard knot in the Boliver's tail.

"Now, I shall eat you both up," the Boliver howled.

"Silly," Raggedy Andy said to the Boliver. "How can you eat us up, even if we should let you? If you swallowed us, you would be eating us down."

"I guess I can stand upon my head if I want to when I eat you. Then I would be eating you up."

"Oh, you could if you wanted to, I suppose," Raggedy Andy said as he tried to think of a way to keep the Boliver from eating him. "But it would be very uncomfortable for you to stand so long upon your head. Besides, unless you run very fast you will never catch your breath."

"That's right," the Boliver agreed as he started running. "Just as soon as I catch my breath, I will return and eat you up."

"I shall not wait for you to return," the knight called after him although his knees were shaking and his teeth were clicking together.

"Do not be so frightened," Raggedy Andy told the knight. "The Boliver can never catch his breath as long as he is running, for the harder he runs the more he loses his breath. And besides, maybe he will forget all about us if he runs far enough."

"I hope so," the knight said very faintly. "Perhaps we should get upon the magical wooden sword and ride away, just in case the Boliver should not forget to return."

Raggedy Andy was just about to agree to this when back came the Boliver running towards them.

"Oh, deary me!" the knight wailed as he sat down on a log. "I knew he would be back."

JOHNNY GRUELLE

The Boliver looked as though he would run right into Raggedy Andy as he came up, *lickity-split*, but Raggedy Andy did not budge, so the Boliver stopped right in front of Raggedy Andy. "You fooled me, Mr. Raggedy Andy," the Boliver panted. "The more I ran, the more I lost my breath. And, I'll bet a nickel you knew it all the time." And the Boliver sat down upon the log beside the knight and puffed and puffed until he had caught his breath.

"See there," he said when he stopped puffing, "now, I have caught my breath, so I shall eat you up or I shall eat you down. It makes no difference. You can draw straws to see which I shall eat first."

"I don't want to play," the knight said. "I've got King's Ex."

"Ha! King's Ex," the Boliver laughed very rudely. "King's Ex doesn't count. We are not playing that way. Get two straws and draw. The one who gets the shortest straw must be eaten first." The Boliver crossed his legs and leaned back comfortably while he waited for Raggedy Andy and the knight to draw straws.

Raggedy Andy prepared two straws and said to the Boliver, "The one who gets the shortest straw has to be eaten first. Is that what you said?"

"Yes, yes, yes!" the Boliver shouted much louder than was necessary. "Hurry up and draw. I am getting hungrier and hungrier every minute."

So Raggedy Andy held out the straws and the knight drew one.

"Now let me see which is the shorter," the Boliver cried.

First he looked at the knight's straw and then at Raggedy Andy's and sat and scratched his head, for, both straws were the same length.

"I guess I shall have to eat you both at the same time for both straws are the shortest," the Boliver said.

"Indeed they are not," Raggedy Andy cried. "Both straws are the *longest!* So that means you can't eat either of us."

The Boliver took off his hat and thought a moment. "You will have to draw again," he finally said as he held out the same straws. But of course the straws were still the same length when Raggedy Andy and the knight drew again.

"I can't understand it," the Boliver cried. "But I know if the straws are the same length they are both the shortest, so I shall make a sandwich out of you both and eat two of you at once." So the Boliver pulled a lot of leaves and put them between Raggedy Andy and the knight.

"I guess I will start with their heads," the Boliver declared aloud.

"You forgot salt and pepper," Raggedy Andy cried.

"Ah! Who cares for salt and pepper?" the Boliver cried.

"I wish you would not act so silly," Raggedy Andy cried as he brushed the leaves from between himself and the knight. "You know perfectly well you cannot make a sandwich out of us."

"I'd like to know why not?" the Boliver asked in an injured tone. "Didn't I promise to eat you? A Boliver always keeps his promise."

"How can you eat us, Mr. Boliver, when we are as large as you? Don't you see? If you ate either one of us it would make your stomach ache like the dickens?"

Raggedy Andy sat down upon the grass and laughed and laughed.

"I don't see anything funny about being eaten. Do you?" the Boliver asked the knight.

"No, I don't," the knight replied. "And what's more, I don't want to be eaten."

"Well, then, stop shaking," Raggedy Andy told the knight. "The Boliver can't eat us, because he has no mouth."

Of course the knight had not noticed that the Boliver had no mouth and the Boliver had not told him.

"If you hadn't noticed I didn't have a mouth, I'll bet I could have eaten you in three shakes of a door knob's tail."

Raggedy Andy and the knight rolled upon the ground and kicked up their heels as they laughed at the Boliver. And this made the Boliver so angry that he came over and sat down upon them.

Of course this did not hurt either Raggedy Andy or the knight, but after awhile they grew tired of having the Boliver sit upon them, so they rolled over and sent the Boliver tumbling upon his back.

Now, when a Boliver is upon his back with his legs kicking up in the air, he is almost as badly off as a turtle.

When they had let him kick around for a few minutes, Raggedy Andy and the knight set the Boliver upon his feet.

"Well!" Raggedy Andy said. "Here comes our old friend the Snarlyboodle."

When the Boliver saw the Snarlyboodle coming, he did not wait to say good-bye, but went scampering off into the woods, *lickity-split.*

"Why didn't you hold the Boliver until I got here?"

the Snarlyboodle asked. "I wish to paddywhack him for frightening the giant and the little children."

When the giant saw the Boliver run away, he came out of the cave and shook hands with the Snarlyboodle. "I am always afraid the Boliver will bite me," the giant told his friends.

"Then," Raggedy Andy laughed, "you need never fear again. For the Boliver has no mouth."

"If that is the case, then I can easily catch the Boliver for you, for I can run very fast," the giant said.

"You had better start right away," Raggedy Andy told the giant, "because the Boliver was running very fast when he left here."

So the giant ran fast, too, and soon he came back, carrying the Boliver. The giant brought the Boliver up to the Snarlyboodle.

"Now," the Snarlyboodle cried as he waved the paddle, "will you promise never to frighten the giant and the children again? When you promise, then I shall give you a paddywhacking."

"Wait," Raggedy Andy said. "It wouldn't be right to punish the Boliver after he has promised to be good, would it?"

"Let us try kindness with the Boliver," the giant said as he handed the Boliver a cream puff.

"That is a very nice way to do," the Boliver decided as he wiped the tears from his eyes. The Boliver put the cream puff into his pocket. "My! That was good!" he said.

"You put the cream puff in your pocket," exclaimed the knight.

"Of course," the Boliver replied. "My mouth is in that pocket." And although it was hard to believe, the knight found this to be true, for when the knight put his finger into the pocket, the Boliver bit him—though not very hard.

"I guess we had better be getting on to my house," the knight finally said. "It's growing late, and we have been here almost thirty minutes."

The giant suggested that he would run to the knight's house and bring back the knight's wife, but Raggedy Andy thought the giant might frighten her.

So Raggedy Andy and the knight got upon the magical wooden sword and without further adventure reached the knight's house.

Mrs. Knight was a pretty lady and she told Raggedy Andy that she would return with him and the knight to the castle of mean old King Growch. Of course the knight's wife could not ride upon the wooden sword for it was too small for three people to ride upon. But the knight brought out a nice little wagon and that was hitched to the magic sword. It did not take long to reach the giant's cave and when they got there, they found the giant and the Snarlyboodle and the Boliver all ready to return with Raggedy Andy to the castle.

"I believe we will make better time if I carry all of you," the kind giant suggested. So he put on a coat with large pockets and the knight and Mrs. Knight and Raggedy Andy rode in one pocket and the Boliver and the Snarlyboodle rode in the other pocket until they came to the lovely castle.

CHAPTER SEVEN
THE HAPPY ENDING

WHEN the giant, carrying Mrs. Knight, Mr. Knight, Raggedy Andy, the Boliver and the Snarlyboodle reached the castle grounds they found the king and all his guards lined up. And they all had large swords and spears.

"What do you want, old Mr. Giant?" the king asked He did not see Raggedy Andy in the giant's pocket, but though he had never seen a giant before, he felt certain that the giant had come to capture the castle.

"I have come to capture the castle," the giant cried so loudly it made the trees shake.

"You had better run home to your mama," the king yelled as loudly as he could. "We shall never let any old giant capture our castle." And the wicked king ordered all his soldiers to charge the giant.

The king stayed behind as generals do in the armies and let the soldiers do the fighting. Anyway, all the

86

soldiers rode their horses lickity-split at the giant, and would have cut the giant's stocking with their swords and spears if the giant had not been too quick for them. He reached over and pulled a great bushy tree, right up by the roots; then he used the tree just like a broom and swept horses and soldiers head over heels back towards the place where the wicked king stood.

"Ha!" the king cried more loudly and fiercely than ever; "it isn't fair for you to sweep my soldiers and their horses about, so I shall take the tiny bottle which was given me by Winnie-the-witch and I shall call the giant from the bottle to fight you."

"Pooh," the giant replied. "How could you have a giant in that little teeny-weeny bottle?" But just the same the giant drew back a little and waited.

The wicked King Growch took the little bottle from his pocket and tried to open it. "It is sealed with glass," he cried. "How shall I open the bottle and let the giant out?"

"Maybe you will have to break it over a stone," one of the soldiers told him.

"Now you had better watch out if you know what is good for you," the king yelled at the giant as he jumped from his horse and ran over to a large stone.

The wicked, mean king raised the little bottle and dashed it upon the stone. There was a loud *boom* and a cloud of smoke went sailing over the castle towers. Everyone nearby fell over backward. But when the smoke cleared away, the king was nowhere to be seen. He had completely disappeared. There was just a large hole in the ground where the stone had been a moment before.

87

"Where is the king?" all the people asked.

"Ha, ha," the giant laughed. "Perhaps the giant in the bottle carried him away."

"We are glad that he has gone," all the soldiers cried. "He always gave us hard thumps and was mean and cross to everyone." The giant took Raggedy Andy and Mr. and Mrs. Knight and the Snarlyboodle and the Boliver from his pockets. "Hurrah," all the people cried, for by this time everyone had come hurrying from the castle to see what had made such a loud noise.

"Hurrah, hurrah, let us make Raggedy Andy king! Whee, whee, King Raggedy Andy!"

Raggedy Andy, however, held up his rag hand and said, "Thank you very much. I do not wish to be a king. Nor will the giant here harm anyone. He is a very kind-hearted giant and has come with me to rescue my friends from the wicked king's prison coop. Now that the mean old king has disappeared let us all go in and see Raggedy Ann, for she has a magical candy heart and a wonderful Wishing Pebble and always knows just what to do."

So they all went inside the castle except the giant who was too large to get in the doors. The guards brought Raggedy Ann and the witch and Noodles, the donkey, and the Prince and Lovey Lou to the large throne room.

"Well, Raggedy Andy, we see you have had good luck," Winnie-the-witch said.

"Oh, yes," Raggedy Andy replied. "That reminds me that all of my good luck was due to the Lucky Penny, so now I shall return it to the Prince."

And Raggedy Andy handed the Lucky Penny to the Prince, who was standing with his arm about Lovey Lou.

"Did you say Penny, Raggedy Andy?" Winnie-the-witch asked as she ran to the Prince. "Why! It is the charm! It is the charm! You are Prince Bonnie whom the wicked king took out in the woods and lost," Winnie cried as she took off her false nose and hair and threw her cloak from around her shoulders.

Then the Prince put his arms around Winnie and they kissed each other.

"Dear me!" Raggedy Andy whispered to Noodles, the donkey. "Look at Lovey Lou. Her eyes are filled with tears. I was hoping that the Prince . . ."

"Oh! So was I," the donkey replied sadly. "Lovey Lou is very unhappy."

It was only for a moment. Winnie, with her arm around the Prince, held up her hand for everyone to be very quiet; and then everyone heard the lovely melodies from the singing violins as Winnie spoke. "This is your Prince whom the wicked General Growch lost in the deep, deep woods. At the same time, he lost his memory. But now, thanks to the Raggedys and the Lucky Penny, we can recognize him and he has found his memory."

"Hurrah! Long live Prince Bonnie," all the people shouted.

Then the knight's wife said to Winnie, "And you are the Princess Winnie, my sister. Isn't it strange that we should have lost our memories, too?"

Then Winnie kissed Mrs. Knight and asked the Prince for the Lucky Penny. When Winnie took the Lucky Penny, she made a sign before the knight's helmet and the knight regained his memory too.

"Why," the knight cried in a bewildered sort of way,

"I remember now. I went out into the woods to read a book one day, and, as I sat under a tree, an acorn fell upon my head. And I forgot that I was a king and everything."

Just then there was a lot of shouting outside the castle and the giant's voice could be heard above all the rest singing a marching song.

And the great doors opened and here came all of the ladies and gentlemen of Prince Bonnie's court. And behind them came all the children from the giant's cave. Oh, it was a wonderful sight to see so much happiness!

And while everyone was laughing and talking a blue light came upon the throne. And as a hush settled over the great room, the blue light changed to white and there stood the loveliest lady with shiny golden hair.

And in her hand she held a golden wand.

"It is the lovely witch who helped us," Raggedy Andy cried.

"Yes, Raggedy Andy," the lovely lady said, in a voice as soft and sweet as lovely silvery bells. "I am at times Wanda-the-witch. But my real name is Sylvia." And she waved the magic golden wand. "Now," she said, "let us all be happy because the wicked Growch is no more. And let us give thanks to Raggedy Ann and Raggedy Andy for their assistance in helping us. For I must tell you, without the help of Raggedy Ann and her candy heart you would never have found the magical charm, the Lucky Penny. And, without the Lucky Penny we would not have found everyone's memories, for the wicked Growch had a secret potion which he had given

the Prince and everyone whom he did not wish to remain here in the castle. The knight and his wife are the King and Queen of the red castle and Lovey Lou is their daughter, the Princess."

Then lovely Sylvia touched Noodles, the donkey, with the golden wand and the donkey head disappeared and there he stood, a young and handsome man, the same age as the Prince.

"The donkey is Lovey Lou's brother, Prince Donald," said Sylvia.

Immediately Lovey Lou and Prince Donald ran to the knight and his wife, the King and Queen of the red castle, and they hugged and kissed each other.

Then Prince Donald took Lovey Lou's hand and led her to Prince Bonnie and then he took the hand of Princess Winnie and stood beside Lovey Lou and the Prince. And the King and Queen of the red castle raised their hands and said, "Bless you!" while the singing violins played the loveliest of mystic melodies.

Raggedy Ann and Raggedy Andy were so filled with happiness, it seemed as if their cotton-stuffed insides were filled with golden sunshine instead of nice, clean white cotton, and their cotton-stuffed heads were full of lovely sunny thoughts.

Then, Prince Bonnie walked over to the Raggedys and spoke: "Lovey Lou and I have been talking it over and we think you two should have the magical Lucky Penny."

Raggedy Ann and Raggedy Andy replied, "Oh, no! We just found the magical Lucky Penny in the deep, deep woods, but it really, truly belongs to you."

"But, I wish you to have it," Prince Bonnie laughed, "for it has brought us all so much good luck and happiness, I want it to bring you good luck and happiness, too."

"Dear me," Raggedy Ann smiled. "Raggedy Andy and I are just filled with happiness. If we were any happier perhaps all the stitches would rip out of our cotton-stuffed heads."

Then the lovely Sylvia walked down from the throne and said, "Take the magical Lucky Penny, Raggedy Ann. With your candy heart with the words, *I Love You*, printed upon it, you will find good use for the Penny."

So Raggedy Ann took the wonderful Lucky Penny and said, "Thank you, very much. I shall make a wish, that this Lucky Penny shall grow into a Lucky Penny tree. Then, when anyone comes along who is kind of heart, considerate and generous, they may shake the tree and a Lucky Penny will fall down to them."

And everyone cried, "Raggedy Ann always thinks of the nicest and most unselfish things."

So Raggedy Ann took the magical Lucky Penny out to the castle yard and planted it, and there grew a large tree just covered with Lucky Pennies.

The lovely Sylvia waved her wand and made a splendid cave right in between the castle of Prince Bonnie and the red castle of the knight-king and queen. For the giant wanted to be close to all the children who had lived with him so long, and of course the children wished to be near the nice, big-hearted giant.

While all this was happening, a great banquet was prepared in the great banquet hall of the castle and everyone ate and danced and had the gayest and happiest time you can imagine.

And very soon—even before Raggedy Ann and Raggedy Andy left the wonderful castle—there was a great wedding, a double wedding, for Lovey Lou and Prince Bonnie, and for Princess Winnie and Prince Donald. And the celebration lasted a long, long time.

In fact, they are still celebrating, for when love fills our hearts, happiness is everlasting.

And what happened to little Ponko, the puppydog?

Oh, Ponko lives in the castle with Lovey Lou; and in one corner of the garden, Ponko, the puppydog, has a wonderful magical Weenie Bush, for that was the first thing Ponko wished for when Raggedy Ann tied to his jewelled collar one of her magical, good luck,

LUCKY PENNIES.

THE END

Look for these other Raggedy Ann Books

MY FIRST RAGGEDY ANN